Not Totally Unbelievable

Vibhuti Bhandarkar

First published in India 2011 by Frog Books
An imprint of Leadstart Publishing Pvt Ltd
1 Level, Trade Centre
Bandra Kurla Complex
Bandra (East) Mumbai 400 051 India
Telephone: +91-22-40700804
Fax: +91-22-40700800
Email: info@leadstartcorp.com
www.leadstartcorp.com / www.frogbooks.net

Marketing Office:
Unit: 122 / Building B/2
First Floor, Near Wadala RTO
Wadala (East) Mumbai 400 037 India
Phone: +91-22-24046887

US Office:
Axis Corp, 7845 E Oakbrook Circle
Madison, WI 53717 USA

ISBN 978-93-81576-65-6

Publisher and Managing Editor: Swarup Nanda
Books Editor: Oswald Pereira
Design Editor: Mishta Roy

Typeset in Book Antiqua
Printed at Repro India Ltd, Mumbai

Price — India: Rs 95; Elsewhere: US $4

Dedication

This book is dedicated to my late mother and my late father-in-law, the most magnificent and enchanting story-tellers I've ever known.

About the author

Vibhuti Bhandarkar was born and brought up in Mumbai, India. A graphic designer and copywriter by profession, Vibhuti is a passionate and prolific writer. She discovered blogging in 2006 and found it to be a fantastic tool for honing her creative writing skills. A doting mother to an extremely naughty two-year old son, Vibhuti has not let go off her pen and keeps her MoJo intact. Numerous accolades and awards from fellow bloggers and writers from around the world, has strengthened Vibhuti's belief in her pen.

'Not Totally Unbelievable' will be her first published collection of fiction short stories book for young adults. She is currently working on a novella and you can reach her at vibhuti.bb@gmail.com

Contents

At the Lingnan Tea House

Liu and Lin were staring blankly, out of the wide kitchen window with frail timberwork which gave a broad view of their back yard. Farther beyond the peony shrubs that lined their courtyard, Liu could see the vast expanse of the empty patch of land under dispute between the two feudal lords in Guangzhou (Canton). Both had passed away and the land still lay waiting to be claimed by the legal heir. There the tall silk wool tree still stood bare, tall, spiny, cold and would continue to stand so until spring. Not a single of those beautiful, vibrant, red and orange five petal flowers with white silky-cotton in their folds was in sight. The elegant emblem of Guangzhou was still to bloom. Liu felt one with the tree, devoid of emotion, standing solitary in its own steed, on a no man's land but she never mentioned this to her younger sister.

Most of the Chao Chan family members hadn't survived the war and neither did they have their own ancestral home in Fujian. Their father, their brothers had all marched away into oblivion, never to come back. What had come back, in 1937, was the news that the Japanese had trampled all of them in the heartland of

China. Their mother did not live for very many days after, leaving eight-year old Liu behind, lost and lonely, nursing a sixteen month old, Lin. Years later, now with the establishment of the People's Republic of China, they were slowly recovering from their financial, moral as well as psychological set back.

Lin watched her sister's face from the corner of her eyes. Light seeping through the louvers in the top ventilators of the window was banding her face. Lin's teenage mind started imagining it as the war paint Liu might have used to ready herself for combat. Lin noticed that Liu's eyes had that steady gaze. Liu's face would assume a wooden look only at times of grave impending trouble. She was otherwise a very kind and amicable person to be with. Today, Lin was sure that memories and turmoil of the past were resurfacing, which Liu was trying to conceal behind those steady eyes. Lin had never seen Liu shed a single tear that could give away her deepest feelings. Liu had always maintained her composure, coolly tackling all the hardships that came their way while Lin remained a silent spectator, never allowed to be party to any kind of suffering. This time, however, Liu needed all the support she could get.

Lin was brought out of her reverie by the sound of Liu's hands, now working again, mechanically chopping the meat with a huge, sharp knife, on the butcher's island in their kitchen.

"I don't want your complaints if you can't give me a solution!" Liu sternly reprimanded Lin without looking up, regretting it later.

The sisters were now pondering again over the calamity that was to visit them today, predicted a week ago. Lin knew it was time for her to do something.

****

Silver Stream village was a picturesque site, kissing the foot of the mountainous range with a small, melodious waterfall streaming down its western side. The front porch of their maternal uncle Chou Yang's dilapidated ancestral home was often sprinkled by the clear water from the stream. Uncle had escaped to Hong Kong after bringing Liu and Lin to reside here, in 1943.

With the help of some elderly neighbors, Liu had revived their ancestral business as soon as she'd arrived even though she was just a teenager then. ***Cha Dao**, the art of making tea,* ran deep in her blood. After all, generations and generations of her family were at the centre of the massive tea trade that existed between China and Europe during the 19th century. Liu set up her own Lingnan Tea House aptly named after the colonial quarter of Guangzhou it was located at. And six years later it was hustling and bustling with patrons all through the day. 1950 was a very good year for ***Peurh**, aged tea* and Liu was expecting tremendous business.

On the wall facing the doorway, she hung a paper scroll on which was a Tang poem written by Lin in her long, slender, slanting, calligraphic hand that said *"...One bowl soothes your throat. After two, loneliness and boredom disappear. With the third, you will find rising from your bowels enormous volumes of poetry and literature. The fourth bowl leaves you in a light sweat and all of life's despair will seem to be floating away, out of your pores. After five bowls, your muscles and bones are cleansed of all impurities. Six bowls and you will be communicating with the spirits. Beware of the seventh bowl! You may grow wings and find yourself flying with the winds..."*

"Is this communication with the spirits drawing the Cantonese to our tea house?" Liu wondered in proud admiration.

Her personal favourite was the Red Heart Ti Kuan Yin Tea, considered the mother of all **Oolongs**. One king had done justice to the tea by describing it as heavy as iron and as beautiful as ***Kuan Yin,*** *The Goddess of Mercy,* and thus the name was given. This year's tea was not tightly rolled and that meant after the first two brews, the toasty roasted flavour with the rich bready notes would completely open up, giving a warm aroma, bright taste and a comforting feeling to the patron. Liu particularly felt that notes of honey lingered on after the tea was set to brew and there was also an unmistakable soft and heady scent in the air like that of red roses on a hot summer day.

"This Tea will definitely elicit romance!" she had giggled to herself unaware that the same magic of the tea leaves would spell trouble for the sisters the very next day.

****

The Lingnan Tea House seemed like a tranquil oasis that morning. The quaint bamboo furniture and the tinkling sound from the waters of the small fountain placed near the South window, added to the serene and peaceful ambience.

Liu looked on as Lin served at a table with a sharply acquired skill and artistry. She had selected the White Needle Tea and was treating an old customer to cup after cup of the superbly made tea. The full fragrance was wafting across to her and the sweet notes of the white tea were evidently satiating the guest. Lin carefully picked up the covered ***Gaiwan**, the tea caddy,* on its plate with the left hand and placed it on the up-turned fingers of her right hand. The lid was positioned slightly askew and held in place with the thumb, just enough to allow the tea to pour out while retaining the leaves. The tea was then lovingly poured from the pitcher into individual, tiny, tasting cups. Lin was sure to be attentive enough and refilled it when emptied.

The Indian guest who accompanied the old man was happily observing and unable to contain his awe exclaimed, "That's amazing! There's neither a timer nor a water thermometer employed and yet each cup has the amazing consistency of the one prior to it. It's simple, graceful perfection at its unparalleled best!"

At that very moment of exhilaration entered he, who Lin and Liu would dread later. After being dutifully served a series of cups of Ti Kuan Yin Tea by Liu, ***"Yum Cha**, the culture of tea drinking,* runs deep in my veins." boasted Ming Hsien. "We complement each other so well, Liu. What a handsome suitor I will make!" Ming

Hsien had declared to Liu, proclaiming his infatuation for her. This haughty, stout man seated before Liu seemed to be in his late 30's and was laden with Jade ornaments, strongly reminding her of the malicious feudal lords. His eyes didn't laugh when he flashed that toothy smile. A fear gripped Liu's heart at the sight of this admirer because he looked as if he was faking it. The very first feeling at his appearance was that of instant abhorrence and she couldn't fight it at all. Even Lin had mentioned later that she couldn't imagine her demure, petite sister standing besides the husky man at the betrothal ceremony. "His receding hairline makes it worse to imagine!" Lin had bitterly observed.

Ming Hsien had not only proposed love but had also issued a death threat after sensing probability of rejection from Liu. His fiery eyes clearly said that he meant every word he'd spoken. Each word of love was as sweet as nectar but each word of retribution also dripped venom. Before leaving the Lingnan Tea House Ming Hsien had menacingly slammed two freshly minted, coffee coloured, twenty Yuan bills on the cashier's table, promising to return the same day, same time, next week.

Money meant nothing to Liu but their safety did.

****

A week of worrying and despair had gone by. He was to arrive again today. Lin knew she could help her sister. She watched Liu chopping away at the meat randomly.

Liu's mind was elsewhere. She was obviously bothered by the abominable proposal.

Meanwhile Liu was searching for a specific reason to refuse. She knew that turning Ming Hsien down would mean another term of loneliness besides the threat to their lives. "He's definitely not the one!" Liu had finally, bravely decided.

"I have a solution!" offered Lin, trying to sound as convincing as possible. Liu looked up in an instant, searching her younger sister's face for an explanation. "Don't ask me how but I will send him away. You just wait and watch!" assured Lin.

When Ming Hsien entered the Lingnan Tea House punctually, Lin and the tea house staff surprisingly welcomed him. He was astonished at the hospitality and almost celebrated this obvious favorable change of mind with Liu. He was ceremoniously led to the table where the lissome beauty was seated in the choicest corner of the tea house that granted a fantastic view of the building's surroundings. Hsien studied her face, searching for any trace of the bitter hatred he'd seen in her eyes the last time he'd voiced his emotions. Liu had no clue about Lin's grand plan, but was playing along for she trusted Lin's intelligence.

Soon Lin appeared from within, bearing a pot of tea on a tray which she proclaimed had been specially brewed for the prospective couple to partake. "Let us pray to the great Kuan Yin, before you share the ***Tisane.*** However, I warn you Ming Hsien that the spirit of this tea will tell you how your future together will be. That's the power of the goddess of the Oolong and Peurh!" Lin declared in a formidable tone that would display her immense knowledge of the magic of brewing.

Liu had been warned not to drink the tea. The gullible Hsien, very religious at heart, promptly gulped down the first cup of the magical tea placed before him. No sooner had the first swig traveled down his throat than his face contorted to look like a dried prune. He sprung from his seat like a jack-in-the box, shaking his head in mixed feelings of dismay and disbelief and headed for the exit without another word to Liu. When he halted at the door, Lin feared the worst. Would he turn back? Had he realized she'd pulled a trick? He, however, only turned for one last glimpse of the kneeling, immensely beautiful Liu and then disappeared around the bend.

Liu could not control her emotions. For the first time, tears rolled down her cheeks, blazing a red path on the fair skin. She wrapped her arms around Lin out of relief, gratitude and the immense amount of love she felt for her. "...But what magic did you do, Lin?" inquired Liu.

"It was ***Che Dang*** that very bitter tea, dear Liu. Three pearls of the Ilex leaves must have made such a sour brew that he ran away in fear of a future likewise!"

The sisters hadn't enjoyed such a hearty laugh in ages!

Trekking through time!

He was hurtling down, down, down into the pitch black hole at breakneck speed. As soon as his foot slipped, he found himself travelling through a dark tunnel. He seemed to be zipping at such a tremendous speed that he could clearly hear the wind besides him, screeching in his ears, deafeningly loud.

As his body became an object beyond his control, his soul felt torn out of his ribs and from between all this confusion, he could also hear his heart thumping, louder and louder and louder. His mind was also amazingly aware that for the first time in its lifespan it was traveling to an unknown destination, at an unimaginable speed. And yet thinking was easy, not muddled, and memory was still sharp. As he plunged further into the seemingly inexhaustible depth of the space-like space, from where it seemed even light wouldn't be able to escape, Dereck thought, "Am I dead?"

It's said, when death is near, your whole life flashes before your eyes. "...Or maybe I am not dead yet!"

****

All of his recent past was flashing before Dereck's eyes.

Just twenty four hours ago the brightest student of the batch of 2006 was being bullied into taking a break by his peers. Just moments ago, Dereck Henlein was that twenty something, striking yet nerdy, Law student at Bonn University who was always worried about writing his papers and preparing for exams.

Complementary to that was Aditi Rao's carefree attitude that made his heart throb for her. Aditi's tawny, dimpled face with the diamond stud nose ring and chandelier ear-rings peeking from behind the thick curly locks, appeared before his eyes. At the mention of the trekking trip with their roomies, Dereck had expressed his concern about the pending tutorials. She was chiding him.

"You have all the *Vo..Vo…Vorlesungsfreie Zeit* to do that!" Aditi had stuttered.

She'd meant to translate 'the remaining time' into German and Dereck noticed that with great difficulty she had finally attempted to speak a few words in German, aloud and confidently. Dereck was the compelling reason for those language classes Aditi had taken up seriously.

It was Aditi's idea to holiday together before their *'Sommer Semester'* actually commenced. Unlike him, Aditi was more outdoorsy, extremely friendly and had such great energy for life. So the proverbial opposites were attracted to each other. To keep her happy, he had packed for the trek promptly, as instructed by her.

By noon they left their palatial Bonn University campus and headed for the wooded mountain range in Baden-Württemberg. It was a clear, sunny and slightly windy Saturday as they drove through the picturesque South-Western German countryside. "I needn't worry till mid-April..." Dereck had assured himself, "... for lectures won't begin until then". The thermometer in the car was showing 25°C, which Dereck confirmed was accurate since his new wrist watch showed the same.

"Know what guys, I'm mighty proud of this piece because it's got everything in it, Compass, Altimeter, Barometer...you name it! This makes me feel completely equipped for mountaineering." Dereck had exclaimed, gloating over his super-cool, rugged, expedition wrist watch. Dereck remembered that Kurt, Aditi and Sonja had exchanged sneers at his child-like excitement.

"Why doesn't it glow in the dark, now?" fretted Dereck, failing to read its face as he travelled through the dark tunnel. " ....probably because I'm traveling faster than light!" he concluded as he continued to be sucked into the black hole by gravity.

****

Just twenty four hours ago, as per Kurt's itinerary, they were driving south from Freiburg, through one of the first major towns, Sankt Peter, to reach Breusgau, the city closest to the mountain. There they would leave the car behind and in the wee hours of the day, would begin their mountaineering, up to the top of Feldberg, the highest peak in the Schwarzwald or the Black Forest.

"It's 4898 feet to be precise." Kurt had informed while Aditi checked on their supply of mineral water in the boot.

"Wow! Are you ready for this?" Dereck had questioned his conviction secretly, aloud.

"Pardon me?" said Aditi handing Dereck a bottle of water that she'd just opened and sipped from. "Drink some, you look parched already!" she'd chuckled.

Map in lap, as Kurt drove ahead, it was amazing to see stunning vistas of lush green hills and tall trees everywhere one looked. It was like a beautiful color palette to choose from, a range of vibrant and varied hues. It felt as if they were surfing through shades and tints of greens and yellows and reds and oranges. The road wound through the terrain, past the low hills finally entering the rocky mountainous region. The journey was gorgeous at every mile and the drive every bit pleasant.

It was Dereck's turn to prove he was equally knowledgeable as Kurt. "The Black Forest gateau has its origins here. And it's called the Black Forest Mountain due to the dark shadows cast by the innumerable tall fir and pine trees, drowning the mountain amidst the woods, into pitch darkness." he informed the trio.

He watched Aditi's face light up after this newly imparted trivia and he hoped she hadn't noticed his fair cheeks flush a lovely red with glee.

"I'll take you to my home town in India some day. It's as

gorgeous and seductive as these landscapes, too." Aditi had triggered Dereck's imagination with these words.

****

After spending the night at a beautiful Spa-Resort on the banks of Lake Titisee near the foot of the mountain, they had finally set off early Sunday morning on the chalked out trekking trail. At first it looked like a comfortable route up into the volcanically formed topography, a well-marked trail indicated by a rhombus divided vertically into red and white segments on a yellow background.

Gradually they realized that the Black Forest was definitely not a sweet confectionary. The hike was challenging which they had to foot through a cover of sandstone that formed a crusty layer on top of the core of gneiss. The topography was generally steep and rugged, formed by heavy dissection of the substrate by surface water. The dense forest thicket of tall Fir trees didn't allow much light, rendering poor visibility. Kurt and Aditi were lagging far behind, Sonja was climbing just after him and Dereck had surprisingly taken the lead. He was reveling in a sadistic pleasure, derived from seeing Kurt struggle up the rocky side. Dereck had placed one foot at a time, carefully selecting a sturdy crevice, judging the foothold, shifting his weight and up!

"It's amazingly easy!" Dereck had jubilantly shouted out to those tagging behind him.

The rhythmic progress was fast and he'd reached the

top, from where it was overwhelmingly scenic. He was screaming back at the party that was still slowly climbing up, giving Aditi a verbal description of the awe-inspiring sight that lay before his eyes. Lost in his song about the hills, Dereck stepped backwards. The earth at his foot suddenly seemed to heave. Assuming it was a trick of his tired mind he continued standing there. And then the unimaginable happened. The floor of the upland at the peak had given in, letting him drop through. Dereck had screamed his guts out for help but it was too late and now he was flying down, towards the point of no return.

****

As he spiraled headfirst, downwards, the invisible interiors of the black hole, the walls that Dereck imagined the tunnel had, seemed to be heating up. Despite the blinding darkness, Dereck could tell that the passageway seemed to be dilating, widening, for the feeling of space around him had increased. The temperature was rising and hot air seemed to be blowing at his face from the pit, 5000 feet or more, down below. He assumed that the heat was emanating from the molten Lava that may be gurgling at the end of the dormant volcano he had possibly dropped into. He felt as if he was being pushed down, down, down!

And then suddenly bright light hit his eyes. Dereck shut his eyes tight for the white light hurt but he knew he was out, finally, safely. He couldn't help but cry out of happiness for he was out again in the open air, breathing normally, physically unhurt, in one piece.

The landing was amazingly soft. As he slowly opened his eyes everything was blurred and in black and white. Many unfamiliar faces were staring down at him and talking incessantly. They were discussing him. Dereck was simply too tired to keep his eyes open anymore so he resigned to the fatigue and dosed in the warm bed that the kind strangers had put him in.

After a good rest when he opened his eyes once more, his vision had improved but he still couldn't move his body as easily as before. Again a whole lot of new faces were staring expectantly at him and were smiling.

"Why are these strangers so happy with my well-being?" Dereck wondered. He decided not to strain himself and went back into slumber, so that he could recuperate faster.

The next time he woke up it struck him that all the strangers looked very similar to those he'd seen in Aditi's family photographs. And they all spoke a language he didn't understand. "Aditi couldn't have possibly brought me all the way to India after the fall, could she?" thought a baffled Dereck.

He also noticed, like Aditi had mentioned, they were really very hospitable people for they had very thoughtfully also draped a soft, white, mesh-like curtain around his bed. "It's probably a net to keep the mosquitoes or other insects out!"

The house seemed to belong to a wealthy family. The false ceiling above his cot had an elegant, ornate design and the aroma in the room was of fresh lilies. They kept him on a liquid diet.

"I must be still very weak from the fall!" observed a drowsy Dereck and drifted off to sleep once again.

Later Dereck made many more unsuccessful attempts at moving his body or talking or even getting up to go to the toilet but failed. Substantial time elapsed before he found his tongue but what rolled off his tongue was undecipherable to him, too. Gurgling sounds came from his throat which was very different from what he meant to say. However, gradually his condition improved. Dereck managed to move his limbs well and also spoke a few words which he hoped the Indians understood. There were many questions, the answers to which he was desperately wanting to know.

How on earth was he over here, In India, so far away from where he'd last lost consciousness?

Who were these people who seemed to be responsible for his well-being and were doting on him 24/7?

Why was he not being visited by Aditi or any of his old friends?

What did the doctors have to say about his physical fitness returning back to normalcy, completely?

Did his parents know where he was?

And above all since how long was he here?

So one fine morning when the gentle fair face of the

kind lady who had taken good care of him all this while appeared around his bedroom door, he was excited. A sort of happiness would always surge in his heart the moment he saw her. He knew not why. His eyes found solace in this one pretty carved face only. The rest of the household were only company to him. She seemed to understand everything he'd ever wanted to communicate so this time he attempted to ask *"Den Wievielten haben wir heute?"* Dereck clarified, "Meaning what's the date today?"

No sooner had he spoken those few words then her facial expressions changed rapidly. At first she looked shocked and dumbfounded, then she gave a low gasp, her eyes grew large and she suddenly flew out of the room screaming, "He spoke in German!" The alarm in her voice was reverberating in Dereck's ears. He was missing Aditi right now, terribly. Though this lady seemed to speak English fluently he still felt a fear that he wouldn't be able to communicate with all of them, very well. Aditi's presence would have been a great moral support.

The same evening, Dereck awoke from deep sleep only to see a huge swarm of excited and bewildered people right outside his bedroom door. Some of them were carrying mikes in hand, others were with notepads. There were many men with cameras hoisted on their shoulders. They all seemed to want to have a word with him. The kind, guardian lady was seated at the edge of his bed, near the head rest.

A stupefied Dereck was wide awake and sitting up now.

Spotting him awake they were reluctantly let in and just when he was wondering "Are they Reporters? What have I done?" the bombarding of questions began.

The first reporter addressed his lady guardian, "He's just a year old. Are you sure ma'am you heard him speak German?"

While a second reporter was asking, "How many times has the child spoken? What were his exact first words?"

Dereck couldn't believe his ears, "A one-year old? What did that reporter mean? How could they make such a blunder? Are they blind?"

Just then a third reporter continued the interrogation, "Are you sure the baby wasn't just gurgling and you mistook it for GERMAN? For all you know, maybe he'll be speaking in Latin next!"

As the crowd burst out laughing at this mean retort, Dereck came to his guardian lady's rescue.

He repeated, *"Den Wievielten haben wir heute?"* That's exactly what I'd asked her." A shocked silence suddenly fell over the assembled crowd.

And then a voice from the crowd replied, picking the thread of the questionnaire up again, "It's 5 January 2009… but why was that the first thing you wanted to ask child?"

Dereck failed to understand anything of what was being said. "How could that be? Was I in bed for so long?"

he thought to himself but looked up and answered, " .....because I'd fallen into the tunnel in 2006."

A loud gasp went around the crowd like a big wave. The questions were now being directed again towards the lady and also her family that had arrived at her side by now.

"So you think this is a case of a rebirth?"

"Ma'am do you think his past life memory is still intact?"

"Have you tried asking anything more about his past life?"

Dereck was listening to the incessant voices. He slowly jumped off the edge of the high bed and walked to the reflector that a cameraman had placed facing him. Dereck saw the blurred image of a fair, chubby, boy with jet black mop of hair and dressed in a blue playsuit looking back at him.

"This isn't a rebirth, I've just travelled in time!" concluded Dereck, aloud.

What if?

What if I'd not continued to sit on the sofa across her, sensing that she was in one of *those* moods? She sat by the window, rotating the string of 108 *japa* beads. For a fifty-year old, she had a sharp memory. She could verbally paint a complete picture of olden Mumbai before my eyes if only I had the time to patiently listen to her reminiscences.

Mumbai of 1969 was a whole lot different, said my mother. Broader roads, lesser population, more naivety, lesser crime and the list of plus points could go on. Their life had much more meaning then.

"...And we thankfully had all the time in the world to revel in the beauty of that golden era, unlike your generation!" she sighed.

" ...And I could also go on the rooftop to fly kites with the boys " she giggled like a teenager again, as she tripped down her memory lane. I could almost see the adolescent glint come back into her aged eyes at that moment.

A student of Arts at Bhavan's College, she was like many

other teenagers of her times, carefree and a daredevil at times. Young blood was raring to take on challenging tasks head-on. That was how she was brought up to be - a tomboy of sorts. She made quite an entry at college, dressed in a *salwar suit*, designed in the latest fashion. There weren't many girls who would doll up like that in those times. "Most draped saris," said she.

What if I'd feigned fatigue and excused myself out of the room right after dinner? One story from the horse's mouth would have gone untold. But I didn't, and she continued telling a tale that had changed her forever.

****

After switching many homes, my mother had spent her teens at an apartment complex near the Impala Auto spares building, neighboring the Great Royal Opera House. King George V had inaugurated the Opera House building in 1911, which had been completed in 1912. With cinematography gaining popularity in the thirties the Opera House was modified to screen films.

The Opera House was built in baroque design featuring a blend of European and Indian architectural style. My mother was proud to live close by such a magnificent structure that lent such an imposing view from her bedroom window. Sixties was an era when the Hindi movie industry flourished and had a tremendous influence.She was undeniably smitten by Shammi Kapoor, the tall, fair, ravishing actor with the gorgeous locks. He danced in Eastman colours on the 70mm screen and my mother's teenage heart would roll a rumpus in the pitch dark of the cinema hall. She and her gal pals would secretly bunk class and slip into Matinee shows. Blessed was the girl that she stayed at *Girgaon* in Mumbai, the land of the talkies. There was Metro, Regal, Liberty and many other cinemas around that they caught movies at. Permission from parents for late night shows was a rare bonus.

That Friday they missed the first show, but after a lot of begging and pleading were allowed to go for the last show of the day. "*Mumma,* its Shammi Kapoor in *Tumse Achcha Kaun Hai,*" she'd informed trying to convey the importance of the moment. And just before her mum could have seen her blush while mentioning his name, my mother had added, "....and Babita. Lata Mangeshkar and Mohammad Rafi's singing is fabulous. Oh! *Maa,* you should come along too!" she trilled.

After the show, her friend Meena and she were merrily walking home, reviewing the movie, humming the songs and polishing off their packets of leftover pop-corn. They had to go down the lane past the Royal Opera House. The towering structure of cold Italian marble seemed to be shrouded in quaint silence. It stoically stood there, a symbol of the bygone British era, a dark silhouette against the full moon sky. The trees whooshed and an owl hooted in the distance.

"Very *fillumy*!" Meena had summed up the surroundings precisely in her colloquially accented English. It was indeed an eerie feeling that the girls couldn't shake off. Just before the colourful effects of the movie could drain off their faces, they spotted Munna and another boy standing besides the *kulfiwala,* right outside their building, in the street. Thanking their lucky stars my mother and Meena quickened their steps towards the boys. As they came closer to the duo, the faces were clearer under the dull streetlight and they recognized that the other boy was Bunty, from the house across the street.

What if at this point, they'd not overheard what they had? What if Bunty didn't have that throaty, frog-like, gurgling voice that never missed drawing attention? In the silence of the night, when most had closed shop and not many voices could be heard around, Meena and my mother did catch Munna and Bunty's trailing line of conversation. And they were drawn to the duo out of curiosity.

They overheard, Bunty saying "You got to believe me! Everyone is talking about it though not many have seen it. For me even the thought is scary, man!"

Munna seemed engrossed in the subject and very convinced too. In fact, he looked a bit shaken.

My mother hadn't failed to notice that the boys had half jumped in their shoes, startled by Meena's sudden voice from behind.

"Hi guys! Please may we know what this 'IT' is?" asked Meena.

"You'll wish you hadn't asked that!" commented Munna turning to face the girls as Bunty went on to repeat his story to them.

My mother, however, stood unperturbed through the

tale. She didn't believe. Pooh-poohing the subject as more teenage ranting, she decided to retire home.

What if she'd believed? What if she'd not walked away with an air of all-knowing pride? Would the following days be different? Would the subsequent events be any different? What if there was more, than what my mother had ever known, out there? There was more indeed.

****

My mother's home was a small yet cozy flat on the third floor overlooking the street. She stayed with her parents and two younger siblings, so the house was almost always full of people. Someone would be wide awake, listening to the late night radio as she returned home. She herself preferred to read late into the night until her eyes couldn't stay open anymore. However, this had been such an exceptionally eventful day with an unusual end that she was very tired and she dozed off almost immediately. The following morning she woke up with a slight memory of last night's conversations but she began her weekend without a care.

"That was a Saturday night and both my sisters had gone out with our parents to attend a wedding dinner and reception. I didn't care much for such occasions, so I was at home alone!" enumerated my mother, as I patiently listened. At this point my interest was heightened. I was amazed how easily my mother could remember every little detail. I was completely wrapped in the narration, so I prodded her to continue.

****

My mother had stood by her bedroom window to take in the cool breeze playing with the curtains. The evening was chilly outside and the night sky, grey with overbearing clouds. That's when her eyes settled on the Royal Opera House again. Usually she wouldn't have given it a second glance but today it held her attention. Meena's late afternoon call that day had refreshed her memory about the tale Bunty was telling everybody. "What if all that he says is true?" my mother did find herself wondering. This thought had crossed her mind not once but many times over and over again, that evening. She thought the silence of the empty house was getting to her, so she decided to switch on the radio. Even that didn't help in keeping that scary thought out. So she decided to do some reading instead. That would keep the devil's thoughts in her idle mind at bay!

My mother's parents were book lovers so there were always ample numbers of unread books on the coffee table in the hall. She picked one up and returned to her bedroom. She resumed her favorite corner by the window, snuggling with a blanket in the armchair. She could easily finish the book within the next couple of hours. She didn't care to switch on the bedside lamp. "The streetlight is sending enough light in for me to read." she thought.

The bedroom had a small balcony attached where her mother had set up her little garden of potted plants. The little white roses were in full bloom and were smelling divine.

"I shared the bedroom with my younger sister who

generally made the rules around the house. One of the rules was that the doors to the balcony would be drawn close at 6 p.m. and the curtains be pulled before midnight," my mother reminisced.

In her absence, my mother had preferred not to draw the curtains, thinking, "A little added light from the streetlights won't do any harm. I'm saving so much on the electricity bill tonight."

The unassuming girl was engrossed between the pages when she heard a soft thud outside her window. Normally she wouldn't have cared, but tonight Bunty's voice had been ringing loud in her ears. It had partially drowned in the novel that she was reading but now again it was all coming back to her. She got up from her seat, wrapping the blanket tighter around herself. She didn't know what to expect but never the less peered out of the window to check what might have dropped onto the parapet? There was nothing! She started to sink into the chair once again.

"What if Bunty's words are true. What if there really is a ghost of a Catholic father haunting our locality? What if the construction of the Kennedy Bridge had really taken the lives of many? After all we did resist the British rule and we did abhor the missionaries. What if that father was accidentally killed in a shootout during the mutiny? What if there was much more to the history of this place than we actually know? What if the Opera House is truly an abode to many phantoms?" So many dark thoughts had travelled through my mother's head, one after another at the same time. She was staring at the pages with unseeing eyes.

Something made her look up from the book in her hand. And what she saw turned her world upside down.

Right outside the wooden framed glass door of the balcony, which she had dutifully closed in the evening, was a silhouette. The dark shadow like figure was staring right at her. My mother still remembered how her mouth had gone dry, her throat parched and tongue speechless. She had to prove to herself that this wasn't just a figment of her imagination. The gutsy lady rubbed at her eyes and stared back at the phantom.

It obviously had NO body. It was floating in grey smoke but the face was as clear as the night sky. A long, pockmarked face offset with sharp clean-shaven jaws and a deep cleft. The high cheekbones and bushy brows outlined those bloodshot eyes that refused to stop staring at her.

And my mother stared back.

The eyes were kind not horrific, as Bunty had described. There wasn't any cape flying around him or even any canines like in the Dracula movie. The phantom almost seemed harmless to my mother. It just preferred to float there, mid-air between her mother's white roses as if lost in the passage of time. It felt like the lost soul was almost looking beseechingly at her. As if distraught, asking for help.

What if it was really looking for help? What if it meant

no harm at all? What if it had seen in my mother's eyes what he hadn't found in others? What if it was indeed searching for someone with the courage to come ahead and the will to understand its plight?

The bedroom was not so big and the balcony not too far. A couple of feet forward and she would have been close to the apparition. My mother's heart was pounding like a thousand hammers, and her eyes had almost popped out of her head. Soon my mother had amazingly collected her senses and she slowly tried to raise herself from the seat. She had bent ahead towards the balcony door and would have gotten close enough to know more but it had disappeared.

As the narration ended, I came to focus my sight on my mother's face. It had drained of all colour!

"It must have all come before her eyes once again!" I thought.

"... And then I'd fainted. I came to my senses only the next morning to see my parents faces peering down at me in bewilderment. I lay in bed weak and tired. The doctor had no explanation to my sudden bout of fits. I never saw the phantom again and never did I have another attack of fits ever again," continued my mother and went back to rotating her *japa* beads.

She closed her eyes as if the 'Do Not Disturb' sign had gone up.

She had retold the experience of a lifetime!

A tryst with Cyclophobia

"Aagya Baitan, Telya Masaan, Jantar ki Khopdi, Bhaisasur!" This deep, throaty, ominous sounding chant rented the chilly evening air on the patio of our sprawling farmhouse. With still, undisturbed eyes like poached eggs, the twenty and odd, mix of gurgling tots and chatty adults watched the enthralling performer in rapt attention. It was Daddy, at his elemental best, performing his famous magic tricks. Only the knowing knew that the fearsome mumbo-jumbo was a random mix of irrelevant Hindi words personally coined for pure entertainment. This was the highlight of the weekend merry-making, where Daddy's fan following of relatives would huddle together and enjoy to the hilt.

Daddy was a people's person alright! He once draped a colorful red *sari* and even talked some of his cousins to don their wife's *saris* too. Then they danced that famous jig *'Mere Angne Main'* with swaying hips and lip-synced to the music with red rouged lips. Just like it was right out of that Bollywood movie and had their audience in splits.

Daddy could stretch to the limits in playing host at his party. Well, so giving was Daddy that his relatives had not spared even borrowing his air-conditioner for good.

This lanky septuagenarian's company was of wholesome goodness and there wasn't a single visitor's soul who would not vouch by that. Even the ladies of the family always picked a tip or two from this culinary creative genius. With his knack for cooking up a sumptuous menu, all that his kitchen dished out was lapped up within nanoseconds. From Prawn starters, followed by soup to the main course and a yummy caramel pudding for dessert, was all gobbled up as soon as it was served at the table.

Lovingly addressed as 'Daddy' by the youngsters of the clan, my father-in-law also went by the nickname 'Bhavaji' which means respected brother-in-law in Konkani (a widely spoken language along the south-western coastal belt of India.). Taking the old highway from Mumbai and mid-way to Pune you could drive-in to our haven. And it was most likely that you'd find the lovable Daddy perched on his bucket swing, his throne of sorts, on the patio, if its day. By night you'd find him before the television set. He hardly slept. He'd spring up and out of his reverie to warmly greet you with open arms, all smiles. Friends were more than welcome any time of the day or night, rain or sunshine.

On one lazy Sunday afternoon, came on his old moped, Mr. Gulrajani, his old friend from Talegaon. "*Arrey Tu*?

What a pleasant surprise! Come in, come in!" Without wasting time on exchanging pleasantries, the dear old Sindhi got to business. "Let's go get some meat. My taste-buds are longing for your spicy curry in this chilly weather." And that was what Daddy dreaded the most. "*Argh*!" thought Daddy, "I don't mind the shopping, but the ride on his wobbly M80. Save me, Lord!"

Daddy could feel his knobby knees go weak even at the thought of pillion riding. Before the journey could even begin, a pearl of sweat tickled Daddy's brow. Daddy reluctantly straddled the mount while his feeble pleas went unheard. Daddy's pride kept him from vehemently speaking up about his fear of riding bikes. The motor purred to life once again and the twin riders were off.

The speed at which they were moving, Daddy could have easily walked right beside Mr. Gulrajani and his bike to the station. Trembling knees et al, the duo finally made it to the Lonavala Mutton Shop. Slicking back his tousled silver hair, the pilot of the M80 got off and immediately asked Daddy to excuse him, stepping away for a quick smoke. A not-so-surprised, but irked Daddy proceeded to pay for the meat.

Like a glimpse of the sun from behind water-laden dark clouds, a bright thought dawned on Daddy. He felt a sudden assurance rise in his heart. "The speed at which Gulrajani was riding his *phutphutiya,* a fall is certainly not something I need to fear," said Daddy to himself.

Now, smiling like a valiant hero, Daddy was ready to start the journey home with new-found self-confidence.

He was happy that he hadn't forgotten to wrap a muffler around his neck and his ears were safely snug in the thick woollen monkey-cap. As they drifted past the *toll naka,* Daddy closed his eyes, face turned up to the clear blue sky he was enjoying the cool mountain breeze on the contours of his wrinkled face.

Only when he opened his eyes again, things were different! Neither was Gulrajani nor he on the bike. A crowd had gathered around them and were peering down in bewilderment at Daddy.

"What does Gulrajani mean by coming so close and breathing heavily down my collar?" thought a befuddled Daddy and as he tried to turn around to take a look at his nosy friend, he was jolted back to his senses.

"We had a fall?" Daddy inquired with Gulrajani while he was being helped back to his feet. "How?" Daddy continued to ask but there was no answer.

"Like it is God's decree, my bike journey mysteriously always ends this way!" a nonplussed Daddy thought aloud.

The crowd dispersed as quickly as it had gathered. And the duo was left to their fate, pushing the remains of the two-wheeler home, in weary silence.

The matchmaker

With bitter, metallic smelling hands she cradled my chin. She must have opened that creaky window just before we rang the doorbell. She was now keenly scrutinizing the contours of my face, from mole to dimple, with her crowfeet cornered eyes. I spotted the black crow perched on the window sill, eying me too. On an impulse, I found myself becoming more alert and attentive. Was it just me or did I really see a resigning scowl lurk in the corner of her smile?

Did she like me or did she not? Now was this old spinster going to decide the future of the prospective couple seated in awkward silence before her? Even my would-be mother-in-law hadn't seemed so apprehensive about me when she gave her nod of approval.

Though we settled down in a thread-bare old sofa she'd pointed to, I had begun to dislike this rendezvous already. Just then she let out quite a loud, half cackle and half snorting laugh. Startled out of my wits, I didn't quite understand the meaning behind it. Her eyes seemed to dance with crazy eccentricity. The ambiguity and anxiety must have started to show on my face because

I suddenly felt my left palm gently held between my beau's warm hands.

He and I were now acquainted for over three months. We did find ourselves very compatible and he had proved to be an extremely charming gentleman. He had accepted me with all my silly quirks and didn't seem to complain at all about my girlish immaturity. We reveled in our contrasting behavioral patterns and thanked God for our matching choices. Our near and dear ones had already written me off as *the* piece that completed the jigsaw puzzle.

I was looking around, as if searching, for one reason why we were here?

The old hag had promptly brought me back to the present with her sand-paper voice.

"Draw!" she commanded. And I drew. A table of nine blocks like those in a Sudoku puzzle was what she'd wanted.

"Arrange the numbers. from 1-9 in any random order, as you'd like, in these 9 boxes," she said, pointing her wrinkled forefinger at the notepad in my lap. My beau was asked to do the same on another sheet.

"Don't peek into hers!" she ordered. He didn't dare!

When the task was done she snatched the paper and devoured the twin charts while we waited with bated breath. As her eyes kept traveling to and from my sheet to his paper, they grew larger in bewilderment. I wished she'd known how to tone down her facial expressions a tad bit. I wished she'd cough up what she'd read in the numbers as soon as possible. I didn't think I could hold my breath anymore.

"Fabulous!" She screamed waving the paper in our faces like a flag. "Fabulous!" she'd summed up our future in one word. As I grabbed the papers back, to try and see what she'd seen, I saw!

The two charts neatly constructed with the series of numbers from 1-9 arranged in random order. These twin charts had turned out to be perfect mirror images of each other.

The crow cawed. She gave a satisfied grunt. The fortune was told.

Unheard

In a girls Convent school, many kids like me were well aware that they were the apple of their parent's eyes and conducted themselves with great pride. And there were also many girls who didn't seem to think likewise about themselves.

Even as a fifth grader I remember, many of my classmates lived in their own sweet dream world, reveling in Barbie dolls and organizing parties at each other's place. However, there were Tehzib, Priscilla, Lakshmi and a couple of others who looked down upon these girls and thought their tastes and behavior were immature. During recess and free periods these little women busied themselves with needles and huge balls of colored wool while the silly girls wasted their time playing Tick-tack-toe. These 'Old Mother Hubbards' clacked away with their needles and giggled away at some personal jokes that were whispered into each other's ears. "Women disguised as kids," was what I thought of them.

Now I think back and realize that the two different sectors of women in Indian society were in the making at that moment. Those other silly girls and I clearly grew up to be liberated women and they graduated to domestication. I met one of them the other day and my doubts were confirmed that they were married away early.

In the varying strata of Indian society, we find women of differentiating mentalities. As a school girl I concluded after serious observation that there were essentially three types of women; the Liberated types, the Domesticated types and the Oppressed-Depressed types.

Yes, there were other little women studying in the same class as me who clearly lived and grew up in a very restricted and depressing atmosphere. Many of them voiced their fears and considered they were lucky to be able to even continue studying in class. Amongst the scores of these shy, coy and insecure girls I'd known at school, Meera was the one who always caught my eye. She was an average student who barely managed to scrape through each exam, scoring minimum passing marks but her sorry face said that she'd always genuinely tried to do better.

Despite being from a middle class family Meera always looked like her financial background was nearing the poverty line. She looked worse with every passing year. She was growing up into a shriveled, lanky, disheveled looking girl. Her uniform hung on her bony shoulders and the flimsy belt at her waist failed to give it any specific shape around her waist. The white collar had turned a deep yellow around her neck while the blue of the dress was just a faint reminder of the original Cobalt blue hue. The dress barely covered her bony knees while her legs ended in worn out socks which were rolled down to hide the holes in them. Meera's canvas shoes were relatively new but a size bigger than her feet which obviously showed that they were hand- me-downs. The school badge and buttons on the front were almost always, alternately missing and she was regularly pulled up during assembly for this discrepancy. Remarks in the calendar must have definitely made her life at home miserable. I could imagine how it must have become a vicious circle by now. Meera's feeble pleas with the Prefect, for forgiveness, undoubtedly went *unheard*!

Our Mother Superior was a very loving but an extremely strict disciplinarian. Once I overheard her interrogating Meera in her office. I just stood transfixed to the floor outside. Meera was being bombarded with a series of questions but the eleven-year old just wouldn't speak up. I could see her through a gap in the partition door. She stood their sobbing away and blowing her nose into a dirty little hanky. Sister Jessica who was standing by couldn't take it anymore and pulled her closer to console her. For a moment I was surprised why they weren't angry with her for standing mum. I was bewildered how she wasn't blacklisted as an impudent child by now for not replying. However, when she came out of the office and I found myself looking at her right in her face, I spotted a blue circle around her left eye and her right arm seemed swollen. It had gone such a deep purple that I'm sure it was broken. Were the wounds inflicted or was it just an accident? No one knew the cause of the bruises. Why did Meera not speak up even when she'd been given a chance? How could she have chosen to have her woes go *unheard*?

Once Meera had been absent at school for the consecutive ninth day. This was a crucial year for us and the preliminaries to the board exams were nearing. We'd got a bit worried for her and I promised our class teacher that I'd check in on her on my way back home.

She stayed on the first floor of an apartment building at the end of Moghul Lane. There was only a thin fence that demarcated the property separating it from the footpath. I stood below her window and called for her and what a sight Meera was when she turned up at the balcony. I'd obviously brought her out from between some household chore for she had soap lather in her hair, on her brow and her chin. I noticed from between the wooden balustrade of the balcony that the legs of her *pajama* had been rolled up and the front of her blouse was sprayed completely wet.

"Good you came around,", she exclaimed then lowering her voice she continued, "Have I missed out on much?"

"Yes, I'm worried you really have a lot to catch up on. Can I come up?" I asked.

"No. Not now. I'll throw you my text book. Could you please mark out the important theorems? I mustn't lag behind anymore in Geometry or I'll fail," said a visibly perturbed Meera.

"Then you'd better throw down your Science-II, Practical journals and History textbooks too because..."

Our conversation was interrupted just then when a huge, dark, burly man, probably her father, had stepped out from behind the curtains onto the balcony to stand beside her. Despite the distance, I could see that he was an unkempt man with dirt accumulated under his nails. His chest behind the yellowing, sleeveless vest was abundant in thick, graying hair which also appeared to be growing in profusion on his forearms. This huge bear of a father was now barking at me, "What do you want?"

His loud growling voice drowned the rest of what I was saying.

He now got a firm grip on Meera's elbow and started to tug at it. Her frail voice begged him to wait while trying to continue talking to me. By now however he'd decided to turn back in and dragged Meera along too. She disappeared within, *unheard*!

Meera had managed to pass matriculation and had also secured admission in the same college where I was going. Life wasn't so hard on her after all or so it seemed. Many a times she'd meet me at the bus stop, waiting patiently books in hand. She seemed to have only two *salwar suits* to wear to college, one yellow with floral print and a plain pastel pink set.

We'd board the same bus and she'd immediately take the seat right beside me. Meera was still not very vocal about her feelings or personal life. So during the bus journey together, I would bring out tidbits and tales from my kitty and she would listen attentively, giving an occasional giggle or monosyllabic response to show she was enjoying. Thus went most of the conversations between us. Meera never looked gloomy. Only her eyes always had that deep hurt look.

However, that Tuesday morning she looked exceptionally cheerful and alert, very unlike the usual Meera. She also boarded the bus before me and dropped into a seat beckoning me to sit down besides her. This was very shocking for me.

Meera started the conversation, " I have a question for you."

"Yes?" I replied, my heart beating faster at the mere hope of Meera finally having found her voice. She was about to speak her mind!

"Why are we here?"

Now that was a profound question the answer to which I definitely didn't have.

"I don't know Meera but why do you ask such a philosophical question? The answer to this can only come from someone who can teach us the Art of Living," I replied frankly.

"I'm just fed up of this mundane routine *yaar*," she said.

"No. I think there's much more to this. Are you hiding something? You can tell me. Is there any problem at home again? I may be able to help."

Now was my chance to reach out to this helpless girl and I was going to take it.

"Don't worry *yaar,* I'll manage. I've lived through much more for the last so many years, a little bit of more trouble shouldn't make much of a difference," Meera had coolly said.

I couldn't miss the slight tremor in her voice as she trailed off at the last few words.

"What do you mean?" I tried to help her open out to me but she didn't.

"*Nah!* Let it be. Tell you some other time. I am in a good mood today. I will think everything over in the library over a book maybe."

"....but what is there that you need to think about. You can ask me. Please let me help you with this, Meera." I must have sounded a tad bit exasperated. She refused and walked off towards her class closing the dialogue with a tight squeeze of my palm.

The next morning we were reading it in the newspapers.

A second year Arts student had jumped off from the fourteenth floor of the skyscraper opposite the college campus, late the previous evening.

I sat at the breakfast table shell shocked.

I couldn't imagine the timid Meera take such a drastic step, into the pitch darkness, into the depth of complete silence forever. It had been a pre-meditated step. Meera had gone forever. Meera had gone for good. Gone into the oblivion, *unheard*!

The guy of my dreams...

2005

I'm seated on a black corduroy upholstered sofa. The intricate floral design on it is now only a faded vestige of the richer, brighter golden it must have been before. The sofa is placed such that I'm seated with my back to the entrance door. "Weird!" I thought, but I figured it must be their idea of making space for all their furniture. There were so many pieces of antique furniture and paraphernalia around that even the spacious 2 BHK flat looked and felt cramped. After I'd rung the bell, Mrs Basu had let me into their home through a small passage way that opened into the hall. I had to carefully weave my way from between a tall, open wooden shoe rack on the left wall of the passage, a footstool, a large wooden chest (whose purpose I failed to understand) and the glass-topped centre-table before I could plop myself down at where she'd pointed.

My eyes followed Mrs Basu till she disappeared behind the thin white lace curtain, hanging in the arch of the doorway. As she passed within, the curtain was held ajar for just that brief moment and I noticed a huge, wooden dining table that seemed to consume almost all of the dining area. As I waited for her to return, my eyes traveled over the rest of the interior décor. The Basu family seemed to have a penchant for the vintage and antiques. To me they were all strong indicators that they didn't want to let go off the bygone times.

The wall to my left that defined the length of the room was adorned with knick-knacks and riff-raffs from various overseas travels, a Nepali *khukri* and guns from the British era, besides the numerous family pictures. I was enjoying my visual treat and just as I decided to get up for a closer look at the pictures, out came Mrs Basu from behind the curtain with a plateful of freshly cut pieces of apple. I was eager to start with what I'd come here for.

****

I was a freelance feature journalist for one of the top newspapers in India.

That week I was working on a Diwali special article which would run in the glossies, the forthcoming Sunday. My editor had asked me to come up with a detailed article that would cover at least five different cultures and traditions of the Diwali celebrations in India.

I'd recently shifted to this cosmopolitan apartment complex and felt so lucky to have made that decision. The Diwali Special article was going to be a piece of cake. I'd quickly covered my Tamilian neighbour, Mrs Aiyer and my only confidante in the society *Gujjuben* Gayatri. My own aunt had supplied me with Konkani

Diwali agenda over the phone. She had then directed me to speak to Mrs Lodha, her best pal who lived in my society too, for their *Marwari* ideas of Diwali. It was only Wednesday and after the interview with Mrs Basu, I'd be ready to type out the rest of the article and submit it way before the deadline.

Mrs Lodha had in turn introduced me to Mrs Basu from the opposite building for the first time and I had no clue of her background information. Tackling elders especially when it comes to discussing religion, culture and traditions gets a bit difficult for me at times. I feared triggering off a debate on some topic inadvertently. "Relax! Go with the flow," I told myself.

Mrs Basu, a pudgy, fifty-something, fair lady with flabby arms turned out to be quite jolly. Disarmingly chatty, Mrs Basu was very accommodative, about my string of questions on the Bengali culture and traditions. She gave me every minutest detail and her eyes seemed to gleam as she described their wonderful *Durga Pujo*. We were enjoying each other's company so much that I never realized I'd started addressing her as *Kaki* (aunty). Some hours flew by and we had now diverted from my subject of interest to her pet subject, her only son.

Those were the days when I was a free bird, literally. And like any girl dreams, I dreamt of a tall and handsome beau. Mrs Basu had elicited those dreams again as she pulled me by my wrist to the picture frames and started explaining every photograph.

"Look! This is one of him fishing at Hampi. Doesn't he have a gorgeous smile?" She'd asked.

"..and this is of us at the Taj Mahal. This trip was his surprise gift to his Pa' and me on our wedding Anniversary. He'd saved up for this out of his own pocket money, the sweet boy! Must have been just 19 here..."

" ..Here, see...He's doing the wheely! This must have been from one of the college road trips. He completed his M.B.A. from Germany." While Mrs Basu continued to pull me from picture to another, I was lost in my own sweet world, already day-dreaming about this hunk and his endearing smile. "Wow!" was all I could say at every glimpse of the twenty-something Vivek Basu, who was looking back, deep into my eyes from one of the Sepia toned snaps with a Cowboy hat handsomely tilted atop his head. As I reluctantly pulled my eyes off him and came back to Mrs Basu, I noticed that she now seemed very distant. Eyes glazed, she was sitting on the sofa, staring into oblivion.

My voice had startled her out of her reverie as I bid Mrs Basu goodbye.

"I enjoyed chatting with you. Do drop in again, some time lovely girl," she'd said.

My head was whirring by now. The article and its completion were of secondary importance to me. I was pondering over the evening's conversations with Mrs Basu, The latter half and Vivek Basu, her handsome son.

Had I made a good impression on her? Is she 'looking' out for her son? Was she hinting at something? I could only think of Vivek Basu all through the night. The article could wait. I assumed he was still in Germany.

"When will he be coming back?" I wondered.......

****

2007

I am sitting at my breakfast table with a piping hot cup of tea before me.

I was relishing every sip as I was suffering a really bad sore throat. The doorbell rang and my cook entered. She was her happy, chatty self after ages.

"What's the matter, you seem especially happy today, Lata?" I asked.

"*Maydum,* I got a new job today. I'll be cooking in the evenings at Mrs Basu's place, the old lady from across."

Immediately the memory of that chatty evening with Mrs Basu all started coming back to me at the mention of her name. How could that handsome hunk have slipped out of my mind completely?

"*Arre Wah!* She needs a cook now? Has her son gotten back? Seems like ages since, doesn't it? " I'd inquired oblivious to its probable effect. When I looked up at Lata after shooting the question I found her staring at me with a shocked look on her face and a scowl.

"*Maydum,* you shouldn't be joking like that about such

things!" Aghast Lata reprimanded me. I however still hadn't fully understood the purport of this comment.

Before I could explain myself, Lata had spoken, "... Fear God *Maydum*, fear the spirit! The old widow's son has been dead for 10 years now. It was a freak car accident when the boys were returning from Shirdi. Though time has lapsed you still wouldn't want to joke about someone's loss and grief, would you? "Taken aback I gave a feeble reply, " ....Never!"

I realized I'd just answered a question I'd put to myself years ago.

A little thing called love...

Atop the water tank on the apartment building terrace they sat, Radha and Champa. About twenty crows were all perched on a line right in front of them. Radha's *Dadi Ma* would often tell them that they had all assembled in attendance to a grand wedding. And little Radha's innocent imagination would go wild. The crow's wedding, she pictured, had it all, from the choir cawing in harmony to the bride in white.

"Would they be flying down the aisle?" she'd decided to ask *Dadi Ma* the next time.

Radha the youngest member of the ten families residing in the apartment building was an immensely pampered child. She loved a particular shady spot on the terrace and that's where you'd find her right after school. Barefoot she'd run right up, a doll tucked under her left arm and her schoolbag in the other. The door flung open and to the left of the huge water tank was Radha's property. The tall coconut tree leaned in from the far left corner of the terrace and its broad shady leaves made a lovable arch overhead. It had markedly become Radha's corner with all her playthings neatly arranged by Champa, waiting for her to come back. Drama *Chachu*, they'd nicknamed him, who utilised the terrace for his theatre rehearsals in the evening,had covered the floor of the terrace with leftover marble bits. Radha was very grateful to him for now her favourite spot remained much cooler even at noon.

Champa was Pushpa the sweeper's daughter and her father was the appointed plumber for their apartments. For a girl hailing from a family that had lived for generations below the poverty line, Champa was very well-mannered, good natured and a helpful soul. She was very attached and loyal to Radha, for reasons God alone knew. However, she always remained within her limits, well aware of her social status or the lack of it. More matured for her age she cared for Radha and doted over her like a nanny would. *Dadi* would often be amazed how each fell into their role of master and genie in an instant. When Radha and Champa were together they chirped like two birds on a branch in spring.

Radha would turn six this winter and Champa must have been just about two years older than her. The lives they led were, however, much different.

That Monday, the first of July, was a dull grey day for Radha in many ways. When she ran up to the terrace as always, rain clouds threatened her with thunder, declaring the clear onset of monsoon. "Aah! Rain, rain, go away. Come again another day. Little Radha wants to play," she pleaded the skies. Today a second voice did not ring in. "No Champa?" she wondered. A little sad, a little disappointed Radha gathered her paraphernalia and went back home.

Yet another evening and there was no Champa again, only the pitter-patter of tiny rain-drops to welcome her on the terrace. A small pool of water now formed at her feet and wet her white socks. She decided to be wise and return home once again.

As she lugged her bag in, "*Dadi*, Champa has disappeared!" informed an exasperated Radha.

"Now, now! Don't get so worried, so soon." *Dadi Ma* tried to veil the concern in her own voice. "Champa must have gotten tired of all your bossing and given up on you," *Dadi Ma* continued, chiding Radha.

"... But at least she should have informed you before quitting your job," laughed *Dadi Ma* trying to relax the atmosphere with a bit of humour. Radha's face still remained droopy, her lower lip projected in a sulk and furrowed brows, all told *Dadi* that Radha remained unimpressed. Her anxiety kept Radha from concentrating at school, the next day. She was sure something was definitely wrong with Champa.

Dadi Ma's intuition said so too but she didn't dare express herself. When Champa didn't turn up the fourth day either, Radha started losing hope and the interest in visiting the terrace. Even the rains left her corner wet and damp which *Dadi Ma* was worried would trigger Radha's cough and cold. So the terrace was best avoided.

A week dragged by without Champa and Radha became a restless soul. She refused to get Champa out of her mind. "*Dadi,* will you ask Pushpa about her today?" enquired Radha as *Dadi Ma* dropped her off at the school gates. "She's probably been hired as a help at some home nearby," assured Dadi. "They need the money, my child," *Dadi Ma* tried to come up with an explanation that could justify Champa's absence. This still did not satisfy Radha.

And almost a month later, one Sunday afternoon, the clouds seemed to part a bit. Radha scampered to the terrace to see the rainbow. It started right in the middle of the sky overhead and seemed to go down towards her favourite corner. As if right at the other end where the rainbow dipped down towards the ground sat Champa. Huddled like a bundle, drenched to the core was Champa, shivering like a leaf.

With a squeal of happiness Radha rushed to her side but could not make much of the expression on Champa's face.

"There's a circle around Champa's left eye now...." Radha had rushed down and reported to *Dadi Ma.* "... which is blue and her lip has been stung by a bee. It's swollen and red!"

They both trudged up the staircase, back to where Champa still sat, rocking to and fro. Bundling the little girl up in a warm blanket, they walked her down to their home. *Dadi Ma* started her enquiry in her lilting lullaby voice after putting a bowl of steaming hot tomato soup before her. Without a word Champa gulped it down to the last drop very hungrily. Life and her manners now seemed to slowly come back to Champa. She managed a feeble "Thank you!" and her bloodshot eyes meant it.

"Look *Dadi*," screamed little Radha, "She's got ugly marks now all over her hands and legs. They weren't there before." This sight had deeply pained Radha and she stood there staring at Champa in shock.

Dadi Ma noticed that Champa was badly burnt. Some marks on the legs and hands were not so fresh, some dry and flaky. Moved to tears, Radha gave Champa a tight hug. Champa bathed, changed into fresh clothes, in silence. More food that was offered was gratefully accepted, all with shaky hands and eyes that continued staring aimlessly at the floor. That night Champa must have slept a sound sleep after ages because she pulled the blanket right over her head and snored loudly from within. And Radha giggled. Radha was happy to have her playmate back.

Radha announced at the dinner table, in the tone of finalization that her mother would use with her, "Champa will live with us now onwards. We will put her in a nice school and she will study with me. I'll give her my clothes and toys. And we will all stay happily together, forever and ever."

Little Radha simply knew that one didn't actually need a magic wand to change the life of this Cinderella she knew. She simply knew what was needed to be done to save someone she loved.

Ninny

Nitin was very much like other boys of his age, curious, talkative but the only difference was that Nitin was more of a simpleton at heart. *Aai* lovingly called him *Ninny* that stuck with him at school, between friends and teachers too. The English teacher of the VIth D at Saraswati Vidyalaya, Srikant Sir, could not repress a smile each time the mother addressed her son as *Ninny*, before him. For Srikant Sir, this little boy's pet name couldn't have been more apt. He thought of Nitin to be no less than a fool.

Even the Geography teacher, Pramila Ma'am found *Ninny* an intolerable, ignoramus, know-nothing. She saw no hope of Ninny becoming anything worthwhile in life. Once Pramila Ma'am had taken up the chapter 'Formation of the Earth's continents' in the Geography period and had just begun explaining,

"In the beginning, more than 4.6 billion years ago, the world was a ball of burning gas, spinning through space...."

Just then *Ninny* had innocently stood up and interrupted the class with his "How do YOU know?"

The white chalk halted on the green board between a

half drawn diagram of the blazing sun and its orbit and the entire class had burst into peals of laughter. One could almost see the hair on the back of her neck, bristle in anger.

Aai, however, refused to accept that her son was any less intelligent than his classmates. She had her own theory that as long as *Ninny* was asking such questions on such complex subjects, it only meant that his brain simply wanted to know more.

At yet another occasion, as instructed by the class teacher to update 'Thought for the Day', *Ninny* had written a quote, in a neat cursive hand at the top of the board.

"I`d rather sink trying to be different, than stay afloat like everyone else!"

"What a thought!" Srikant Sir was clearly impressed.

"And whose profound words are these?" he'd asked.

Ninny walked boldly up to the board and added beneath the quote – ***Shahrukh Khan.***

The very next moment, bedecked with a dunce cap, *Ninny* found himself kneeling outside the class, in the corridor, till lunch recess.

When he went home with a remark in his calendar, *Aai* revolted that the teacher had written off her son as a numbskull.

She disagreed with the teacher and argued, "Taking a good lesson from an actor is not a punishable offense.

Know what *Ninny*, talk sense to a fool and he calls you foolish!"

****

Just about thirty years old, *Ninny* was a strapping young man, well-mannered and good-natured. It was a surprisingly bright day, in the middle of rainy June. And it was an especially superb morning for *Aai* because she was feeling immensely proud on this day. *Aai*'s pride knew no bounds that they'd finally received a confirmation that *Geographical Quick Facts for Class X (SSC Series*) had been accepted and recommended to be included in the latest syllabus by the Indian Education Council. This made her son the youngest author whose book would be a prescribed text for students now on.

There was a frown riding *Ninny's* face though.

"What happened dear, what is disturbing you? You should be celebrating, now that we'll be seeing your name in print, everywhere!" asked *Aai*.

"...but *Aai* read this! Now NavNidhi Publishers and Printers want me to translate the book into Marathi. When I'd approached them with the manuscript of this very same book in Marathi, they'd advised me to write in English, for more profitability and wider acceptance. Now that this book has turned out to be a success, they think, if the same is published in Marathi, it can do bigger wonders. They've asked me to submit, if possible, in Marathi now..."

"Now what's wrong in that? I'm sure you'll be able to do that well too. Your Marathi manuscript must be lying there only, somewhere. You've just got to go ahead and give it the finishing touches. Just give me some time and I'll hunt it out for you." Said *Aai* tightening her *sari paloo* around her waist, poised to work towards taking her son's success to yet another level.

Nothing could wipe that smile off her face today. She felt *Ninny* was being unnecessarily and unreasonably pensive.

".My point is that I can't believe they want the book in Marathi only on afterthought. I could have given it to them in the first place itself."

Just then *Aaba* who was listening in to the conversation until now, contributed,

"An old saying comes to my mind at this moment. Whose words they are, I don't know but some pearls of wisdom they truly make.

As a rule,

Man is a fool.

When it's hot,

He wants it cool.

When it's cool,

He wants it hot.

Always wanting what is not!"

****

Three years later, a letter arrived by courier for Ninny and in his absence, *Aai* opened to read it.

Aai was in tears by the time she'd finished reading the letter. She had read and re-read the letter more than many times before her son got back that evening. *Aai* was more than elated to break the news to him while handing it over. The day of justice was near.

Prof. Nitin V. Nayak had been requested by the Principal of Saraswati Vidyalaya to honor the Annual Teacher's Day function that year by accepting to arrive as Chief Guest. *Ninny's* Alma Mater had called. He complied without a second thought even though the voices of rebuke still rang loud in his ears. His memory brought before his eyes the high pitched teachers menacingly shaking a fore finger in his face. The bullying peers were pushing him, shoving him. They called him names; blockhead, dunderhead, saphead, clown, moron, idiot and the list could go on.

His *Aaba*'s and *Aai*'s words had stayed true. "*The prudent man is less concerned about flaunting his stuff and more concerned about acting wisely.*" And with this *Ninny* had boldly ignored the insolence hurled at him.

"Time will tell!" he'd told himself in those times.

"Indeed." He agreed with himself today.

As he set foot on the same old, cold Kota flooring "You Nincompoop!" reverberated from the past in his ears but as he looked over his shoulders, there were only voices of praise all around him, presently. Eyes followed him in awe. Little girls were standing in a row, from the school gate right up to the foot of the steps and throwing red rose petals at his feet. He was literally walking the red carpet. He was awaited at the top of the steps by a huge marigold garland. He pulled himself out of his past and decided to revel in the present.

Srikant Sir, his English teacher of yester years who was now the Principal of Saraswati Vidyalaya, stepped forward to greet him. The jet black mop of hair sitting atop his head shone in the bright sunlight making it all the more obvious that it was a poorly selected toupee. Srikant Sir was still that pompously dressed man, a tad bit too loud for the occasion. The pot-belly under the well-pressed Lilac silk shirt was complemented by a wrinkled face and sagging double-chin, all clearly contributing to foiling his attempts at concealing his advancing age. *Ninny* could see that time had not made any effect on this man's nature. He was still the same, old, haughty, loud-mouth.

Ninny realized that Srikant Sir was now addressing him and had put his hand out for a formal hand-shake, "This is a moment of great pride to have a star alumnus of the school and the author of a very popular text book amongst us today. It is going to be a very inspiring experience for the children, Professor Nitin."

As *Ninny* put his hand out in reciprocation, it was immediately sandwiched between Srikant Sir's clammy palms. Their eyes met. For a moment Srikant Sir halted between conversations. A look of ambiguity and puzzlement now flushed his face as he tried to recall more about this student from the past.

" ...Professor, I hope you will also oblige us by agreeing to felicitate Mrs Pramila Rao who would be retiring this year. She must have taught you Geography too?" he had continued but was still fumbling with his memory.

"A very much loved and respected teacher she is. I hope you remember her?"

This sentence was ended with an inquiring tone as if pleading for help in refreshing his memory.

Srikant Sir was still the egoist he remembered but he himself was still the simpleton at heart, who could never hold a grudge against anybody.

"Yes Sir! I do remember her clearly and it will be of great pride and pleasure for me too, to be felicitating my Geography teacher!

"..And Sir I must also tell you that it's of immense gratification to be invited back to my school in such a manner. I never imagined I would ever be honored for anything I'd done, over HERE!"

"What do you mean, Professor?" Srikant Sir was obviously shocked at this comment.

"Don't you remember me, Srikant Sir? I'm your very own, little *Ninny* aka nincompoop- the class jester!"

The principal stood there, speechless in flashback.

As everything came back to him, eyes widened and jaws dropped in realization.

The wordsmith

BEST Bus No. 81 arrived. The board above the driver read 'Backbay Aagar' in white paint, bold face, DevNagari script. Another board, very considerately, also translated that into English for those who didn't follow Marathi. 'BackBay Reclamation' it clarified. Suma boarded it absent-mindedly. She did that every day at 7.45 a.m. and was thankful that this bus was mostly always on time too.

Punctuality and perfection marked her personality. She hadn't consciously cultivated it. It was just there in her. Many things about her were like that. Like her ready, bright smile, not intentionally brought about. Her well kempt hair, the spring in her step and a witty retort now and then, all defined Suma.

That day she was exceptionally conscious of another such trait, an uncontrollable passion for good words. One callous glance out of the window from her seat and she saw the Mumbai cityscape throw colours, pictures, messages, offers, all at once at her lost eyes. Advertisements shouted out loud from hoardings, posters, banners, kiosks and gantries. What would catch her attention from the melee would be an exceptionally good word or headline. The beauty of the English language always had her so enthralled that she frequently found herself drawn to her college library and whiling away valuable hours, devouring one book after another.

"Maybe someday I can pursue a career in copy-writing for the Ad world!" she thought looking down at the red Webster's hardbound Dictionary and the little yellow paper-back Thesaurus in her lap. Suma would definitely carry these in her handbag without fail, if she wasn't carrying a novel along. It helped build her vocabulary tremendously.

****

Last week's trip to the library seemed to have changed her, her focus, her world.

Like every other day, Suma had taken the seat at the extreme corner in the rear end of the library, facing the window. That way she ran a lesser risk of being caught bunking class, by a stray professor or that menace called the 'Class Representative'.

Theirs was a small batch of Mass Communications students and that ways they knew all their college mates by their wonderful names. Suma loved the ring to some names. She often wondered whether the meanings of names also reflected in the personality of those to whom they belonged.

Suma remembered herself turning to 'The Cabuliwalla'

from the blue hardbound collection of Shree RabindraNath Tagore's stories. Just then she'd felt the presence of someone standing right behind her. The moth-ball smell of the racks and the damp odor of old pages had suddenly almost disappeared.

"Spicy." Suma had thought to herself. "Musk? Whatever it is, it's heavenly and perfect!" The superbly smelling being had taken the empty seat right besides hers.

"Wow! A handsome guy for once," the devil in Suma's mind had girlishly giggled. Her new neighbour's long, fair, clean fingers seemed to tickle the glossy pages of the 'A& M' magazines.

"I've just landed an internship as an English copy-writer at Lowe-Lintas," he said.

Suma had been startled by his voice. He seemed to have noticed her peeking into his magazine.

"Have to update myself!" the voice continued. Suma had been so enthralled by his personality that she had not realized she was actually grinning back at the guy. She checked herself, wiping away that silly grin.

"Awesome!" She had sheepishly responded, happy that she had found her voice by God's grace. His very presence and then his easy, friendly tone had left her tongue-tied.

However, progressively over the following days they had met, over and over again at the same table and made better conversation, though in extremely hushed voices. She'd learnt his name was Sameer. This Sameer had appeared to be an extremely bright lad and he had that mischievous twinkle in his eyes.

"They call me The Wordsmith!" he had boasted.

Sometimes Sameer would be already seated at the table. He'd sweetly reserve a chair for his junior college-mate Suma. Suma increasingly looked forward to those chance meetings and hated having to leave his side for the literature class she dared not miss.

Suma found herself thinking of Sameer time and again, all through the day, even during class. Suma couldn't bring herself to accept that she was falling head over heels for this guy.

****

The twang of the conductor's bell and the screeching of the tires beneath her suddenly jolted Suma out of her feverish flashback. "Is it love, Suma?" She giggled to herself. "....Between the pages?" Almost proud at the pun intended.

As she stepped down into the present at Peddar Road and slowly walked the pathway to her class she reminded herself that she had to return Sameer's 'Artist's Guild' today.

'He may not take it back but I can't possibly keep it. It seems to be an expensive volume!" With this, Suma headed for the library.

"Isn't Sameer here yet?" enquired Suma to the pince-nez librarian only to be glowered back at. Suma decide to try the senior's class.

"Hey could you ask Sameer to come out please, I need to return this guild, informed Suma to Varun Iyer, the popular CR.

"Sameer Sule is absent today." He replied helpfully.

"No, I'm looking for Sameer Iyer. Is he absent too?" she asked again slowly feeling a sense of anxiety creep over her. Varun just stood in dismayed silence and stared back at her.

Then laughing a horrid laugh, "Is this some kind of a rude joke, junior? 'Cause if it is, life will get difficult for you soon," threatened Varun crossly. Suma was puzzled with the sudden outburst of anger from Varun.

She rushed back to the librarian and pleadingly asked, "I need to return this book to him. Please tell Sameer Iyer I left it here with you!"

The Librarian looked shocked and the colour seemed to drain off her face.

"You've seen him too, The Wordsmith?" the librarian squeaked in a feeble voice. And the book dropped out of her hands. The librarian looked as if she'd faint the next moment. As Suma lifted the book back again, she spotted a scribbling on the page facing the foreword. The message read, "Wish you to include this in the Library in the memory of my late Pa, Sameer Iyer - The Wordsmith!" signed Varun Iyer.

Acknowledgments

From 'The Secret' by Rhonda Byrne one statement has stayed with me. I quote Bob Proctor, *"If you see it in your mind, you're going to hold it in your hand."* However, holding my own published book in my hand wouldn't have been possible if some special angels hadn't also said 'Amen' to my dreams.

My father has been my biggest critic and also a staunch believer in my capabilities. He has been steadily pushing me towards achieving my dreams. I remember, I was just a fifth grader when I first expressed my dream of becoming a published writer some day. Without an iota of doubt in his mind, he'd said enthusiastically, 'Of course!' Thank you, Papa, for being there for me through thick and thin!

Baji, *Mio Marito*, since the day we met I have grown extremely dependant on you and you have shouldered it all, bravely. Egging me on lovingly, you supported my dreams and ambitions. A big thank you for giving them wings, seeing that they take flight!

I cannot forget the love, positive criticism and motivation that some very close blogger friends have constantly given me. Nandini Bhatt, Rumya Bhatt, Deepak Amembal and Karthik K. I will always remain indebted to you all for your valuable inputs that contributed to shaping my writing career.

I had sincerely asked, "Can you set the ball rolling for me?" Heartfelt thanks to Mr Sunil Poolani for that timely 'Yes!' but for you my journey as a published author would never have started, when I truly, madly wanted it to.